Butterfly Buddies

Butterfly Buddies

by **Judy Cox**

illustrated by
Blanche Sims

Holiday House / New York

Library of Congress Cataloging-in-Publication Data

Cox, Judy.
Butterfly buddies / by Judy Cox ; illustrated by Blanche Sims—1st. ed.
p. cm.
Summary: Third grader Robin has a series of mishaps and learns the value of
honesty as she tries to become best friends with Zoey, her partner for a class project
on raising butterflies. Includes butterfly care tips.
ISBN 0-8234-1654-2 (hardcover)
[1. Schools—Fiction. 2. Honesty—Fiction. 3. Best friends—Fiction.
4. Friendship—Fiction. 5. Butterflies—Fiction.] I. Sims, Blanche, ill. II. Title.

PZ7.C83835 Bu 2001
[Fic]   dc21   2001016720

For Teachers
Everywhere

Contents

Butterfly
Buddies

Chapter One

Robin

"Knock, knock," called Gramps.

Robin kicked the covers off and rubbed her eyes.

"Who's there?" she asked.

"Gramps," answered the voice outside her door.

"Gramps who?"

"Gramps who is waking Birdie up for school!"

Robin liked it when Gramps called her Birdie. Robins are birds. He was just teasing.

Mom, Robin, and Robin's big sister, Tamara, lived with Gramps. When Robin was little, Mom and Dad got divorced. Robin missed Dad, but she and Tamara visited him every summer. After the divorce Mom moved in with Gramps. Gramps took care of Robin and Tamara while Mom worked at the hospital. "He takes care of us, and we take care of him," Mom always said.

Now Gramps opened the door and peered in. "You don't want to be late for school," he said.

"Especially not today!" Robin jumped out of bed.

"Not today!" agreed Gramps. He left to wake Tamara. Tamara was in seventh grade.

After she dressed Robin grabbed her pink backpack and ran downstairs. Gramps and Tamara were eating breakfast. Mom sat at the table, knitting.

"Morning!" she said. Robin gave her a kiss.

"Is that my vest?" Robin asked. Mom said knitting relaxed her. In the winter she knitted sweaters. In the spring she made vests.

"Sure is," said Mom. "Stand up a minute, I want to measure it." Mom held up the knitting against Robin's back. It tickled.

"I can't believe how fast you've grown." Mom sighed and shook her head. Tamara's vest was pink. Mom had made Gramps a red one. But Robin's was robin's egg blue, her favorite color.

Mom put the knitting into her bag. She drank the last bit of coffee from her cup. "Gotta go. I'm late for work."

Mom worked as an X-ray technician. She took X rays. Now she grabbed her purse and kissed everyone.

"Enjoy school. I'll see you tonight." Mom dashed out the door.

Robin slid into her chair.

There were butterflies in her tummy.

"Gramps?"

"Yes, Birdie?"

"What was your third-grade teacher like?" Robin sprinkled sugar on her cornflakes.

"Oh, my. That was a long time ago. Let's see. She was a tall woman with a hair net and thick black shoes. Orthopedic shoes, they called them. They had laces and little holes in the toes." Gramps shook his head. "If she caught you daydreaming, she'd slam her ruler on your desk. Made you sit up and listen, that did!"

"How awful!" Robin stopped eating. The cornflakes made lumps in her tummy. "I hope Miss Wing isn't like that!"

Gramps laughed and took a slurp of coffee. "No way, Birdie. They don't make them like that anymore. I'm sure Miss Wing will be very nice."

Tamara took a sip of juice. "I think it's cool you get a new teacher in May. I wish I was getting a new math teacher. Mr. Boston is hard!"

Robin's teacher had been Mrs. Elbert. Robin adored her. But Mrs. Elbert was going to have a baby. Friday had been her last day. The kids in Mrs. Elbert's class had held a big party for her.

Now it was Monday.

Today Miss Wing would be there. She was new to Lake Creek School. Nobody knew anything about her.

"I just hope she likes me," whispered Robin to her cornflakes.

Chapter Two

Red Sneakers

Robin climbed up the bus steps and sat in the front seat. She wore red sneakers. They were high-tops and laced all the way up. She had bought them at a yard sale.

Hippo sat across the aisle. His brown hair stuck up in little tufts. His big front teeth gave him a crooked smile. When he laughed, his eyes scrinched up. He laughed a lot.

Robin had known him since kindergarten. His real name was Eric, but all the kids called him Hippo.

"How come you're wearing those old lady shoes?" asked Hippo.

"They aren't old lady shoes, Hippo," said Robin. "They are vintage shoes. Vintage is better than old. Vintage is cool. What do you know, anyway?"

Once again Robin missed Ashley. Ashley knew about vintage clothes. Ashley had been her best friend—her very best friend—since first grade. Ashley had moved away in January. She promised to write. But mostly she forgot. Now Robin had no best friend. She sighed. Sometimes school was hard. No best friend, and a new teacher to worry about.

When the bus stopped at school, Robin and Hippo joined the rest of their class outside the classroom door. Mike, Allison, Jamie, Brett, and Charly were already there.

"Where's the new teacher?" asked Allison.

"I bet she's nice," said Jamie.

"Well, that's not what I think," said Hippo. "I bet she's really mean!"

Robin shivered.

Suddenly all the kids got quiet.

A young woman opened the door. "Good morning, class," she said. "I am Miss Wing. I'm very glad to meet you all."

Robin took a good look. Miss Wing's glasses had stripes the colors of the rainbow. Her hair was black and shiny. Earrings shaped like birds dangled from her ears.

But best of all Miss Wing had on red high-top sneakers that laced up. Robin couldn't believe her eyes.

"Look, Miss Wing!" cried Robin. "We match!"

"So we do!" said Miss Wing. She winked at Robin from behind the rainbow-striped glasses. "We must be twins!"

She gave Robin a high five.

Hippo was already inside. Miss Wing didn't see him stick his tongue out at Robin.

At math time, he passed Robin a note: "Old ladys wer old lady shoes," it read.

Robin crumpled it up. She wasn't going to let Hippo spoil her day. He couldn't even spell. Miss Wing and she were twins, that's how it was.

"I have the best teacher in the world!" yelled Robin. She ran the last two steps up to her front porch. She flung the door open and skipped inside.

"The nicest, the prettiest, the bestest teacher!" she chanted.

Gramps came out from the kitchen. He'd been baking. His hands were white with flour. He dusted his hands on his apron. Curly black writing spelled out KISS THE CHEF on it.

"So, you liked your new teacher?" he asked.

"Yes!" Robin cried. She flung her arms around Gramps and hugged tight.

"Have a snack," said Gramps, "and tell me about her." They went into the kitchen. Gramps sliced celery into thin sticks.

"Her hair is so long, she can sit on it," said Robin. She slid into her seat. "Only she couldn't today because it was in a hair clip. A hair clip like a butterfly. I want one."

"Put it on your birthday list," said Gramps. He pushed the celery sticks and peanut butter toward Robin.

Gramps always said that. But Robin's birthday was months away. Too long to wait.

"And her earrings are little cranes. Made of folded paper. Ory-something she called them."

"Origami," said Gramps. He poured a glass of milk.

"Can I have pierced ears?" Robin asked. She sipped the milk.

"Yes," said Gramps.

Robin stopped drinking in surprise.

"When you're sixteen," said Gramps.

Robin laughed.

She finished her milk, scooped up her backpack, and headed for her room. Suddenly she turned around.

"I forgot the best part!" she cried. "Miss Wing said we're going to raise caterpillars!" She skipped out of the room and ran upstairs.

Chapter Three

"Third-grade Snots"

The next day Robin wore her red shoes again, but Miss Wing had on black ones with straps. Robin was disappointed. She wanted to be twins again.

I need shoes like that, thought Robin. I'll put them on my birthday list.

Robin sat down at her seat and started to write. Miss Wing clapped for attention.

A new girl stood in the doorway.

"Class, I'd like you to meet Zoey Rhodes," said Miss Wing with a smile.

Robin stared at the new girl.

The new girl didn't look like a third grader. She looked older. Almost as old as a fifth grader. She had brown hair with straight bangs. She had pierced ears. Robin narrowed her eyes. Was that *lipstick* on her mouth?

She smiled at Robin. It *was* lipstick.

Miss Wing led the new girl to Robin's table.

"Zoey, you'll sit here with Robin and Eric," Miss Wing said. Robin couldn't believe her luck. Zoey was going to sit at her table!

"Hi," said Robin.

"*Bonjour,*" said Zoey. "That's French for hello."

Hippo crossed his eyes and stuck out his tongue. "Knock it off, Hippo," said Robin.

"Why do you call him Hippo?" Zoey asked. "He looks pretty skinny to me."

"He's Hippo because he can wiggle his ears. Like the hippopotamuses at Disneyland," said Robin.

Hippo wiggled his ears.

Zoey put her lips together and nodded. "*Quel* weird," she said. "Nice to meet you, Hippo."

At recess Robin hung upside down on the monkey bars. If Ashley were here, she'd hang on the monkey bars, too. All around, kids played with their friends. Allison and Charly played hopscotch. Jamie and Brandon and Mike played baseball. Everyone had a best friend but her.

Maybe Zoey would be her best friend. Robin looked around. But she didn't see Zoey anywhere.

Just then Hippo came over. He climbed the bars next to Robin and hung down.

"Kindergarten babies, first-grade tots!" he chanted.

"Second-grade angels, third-grade snots!

"Fourth-grade peaches, fifth-grade pears!

"And all the rest are great big bears!"

"Am not a snot," said Robin. That Hippo! Always bugging her.

"Are too," said Hippo.

"Am not!"

"Are too!"

"Well, if I am, so are you!" yelled Robin. "'Cause you're in the same grade I am, so there!" She dropped off the monkey bars, smoothed her hair, and stomped off.

That Hippo. Always spoiling something.

The duty teacher blew her whistle. The kids all ran into line, jostling to get a place.

"Watch out!" cried Charly.

"I was here first," said Brandon.

"No, I was!" Allison gave Jamie a shove. Jamie bumped into Mike, who crashed into Brett.

"You're stepping on my toe," said Zoey. She stepped back and fell against Robin.

"Hey!" yelled Robin. She tripped back.

"Stop!" cried Miss Wing. Everyone got quiet. Miss Wing walked down the line.

"We need to respect one another's space," she said gently. "Let's think about how we can do this."

Just then Hippo came running up. He skidded into Robin. She bumped into Zoey, who hit Brett, who shoved Mike, who punched Jamie. Allison knocked Brandon. Brandon fell into Charly. And Charly burst into tears.

Just like when Robin set dominoes on end and tapped the first one with her little finger: *Plop! Plop! Plop!*

Zoey turned and glared at Robin. "Watch out!" she said.

"It wasn't me!" said Robin.

Miss Wing crossed her arms and frowned.

"Class, please go in and get out your library books. Robin, I want to talk to you in the hall."

Robin's stomach felt full of crawly things. Miss Wing wanted to talk to her in the hall. She'd never had to stay out in the hall before, where bad kids waited to talk to the teacher.

It felt like a long time before Miss Wing came out. But it was probably only a few minutes.

Miss Wing folded her arms. Her fingers went tap, tap, tap on her arms. She looked mad.

"Robin," she said. "I'm disappointed in you. I thought you had more self-control. I expect you to set an example for the other children."

Robin felt like she could cry. How could Miss Wing think it was her fault? Mrs. Elbert would have understood. Why didn't Miss Wing?

After school Robin told Gramps about it.

"It isn't fair!" she said. "It was Hippo's fault!"

Gramps took a pan of cookies out of the oven. Peanut butter! Robin's favorite.

"Well, Birdie," he said. "You're known by the company you keep."

"But I don't keep company with that Hippo! I *have* to sit next to him! It isn't *my* idea!"

Gramps set out the cookies to cool. He poured two glasses of milk. One for Robin. One for himself.

"Now Miss Wing won't like me anymore," she said glumly, chewing on a peanut butter cookie. "Teachers never like the bad kids."

Gramps scooped more dough onto the cookie sheet. "Have you told Miss Wing how you feel?" he asked.

Robin sighed. Grown-ups always wanted you to tell how you felt. Didn't they understand you couldn't always *say* how you felt? Maybe you couldn't even *know* how you felt?

She chewed slowly. How did she feel?

Hurt, because Miss Wing should have known it was Hippo's fault.

Embarrassed, because Zoey might think she was a bad kid.

Sad, because she loved Miss Wing and wanted Miss Wing to like her.

How could she tell all that?

Chapter Four

A Caterpillar
Named Marvin

The next day Robin wore her red sneakers
again. If Miss Wing wore hers, Robin would
say "Twins!" and Miss Wing would laugh and
everything would be all right.

But Miss Wing did not wear the red sneakers. It seemed she never did anymore.

Instead she had on brown cowboy boots
with fringe. I want some like that, thought
Robin. I'll put them on my birthday list.

"I have wonderful news," Miss Wing said.
"Our caterpillars came today."

"Cool!" said Brett. He grinned.

"Where's mine?" called Allison.

"Just a minute." Miss Wing laughed. "All in good time.

"Zoey," she added, "would you help me hand out the caterpillars?"

She gave the box to Zoey.

"Allison, you and Brett will be partners," said Miss Wing. "So will Zoey and Robin."

Miss Wing went around the room, pairing up kids. Only Hippo didn't have a partner. "We have an odd number of children," explained Miss Wing.

Zoey handed out little plastic jars. Each jar held some green stuff and a little caterpillar.

When she walked her shoes made little click-click noises. Robin thought it was a lovely sound.

Miss Wing held up a jar. "First, we're going to look closely at this little creature. Be gentle with your caterpillar."

Hippo held his up and peered through the plastic. "Yum! Breakfast!"

Robin rolled her eyes. That Hippo! If only Miss Wing would move him to a different group!

Zoey finished handing out the jars. She sat next to Robin.

Zoey looked in the jar. She made a face. "I don't like worms," she said.

"They aren't really worms," said Miss Wing. "They are the larvae stage of the Painted Lady butterfly. In a few weeks they'll change into butterflies."

"Larvac?" asked Charly. "What's that?"

"That means the baby stage. They'll turn into a chrysalis before changing into butterflies. We'll check them every day," added Miss Wing, "and write our observations in our caterpillar journals."

She handed out folders. "Right now I want you to draw a picture of your caterpillar and write down what you see."

Robin peered into the jar. The bottom was covered with caterpillar food. It looked mushy. It smelled like wet grass.

"Wow," said Zoey. She peeked into the jar. "It's kind of gross even if it isn't a worm."

"I think it's cute," said Robin. "What should we name it?"

"How about Marvin?" said Zoey.

"Okay," said Robin.

Secretly she thought Marvin was a dumb name. She could do lots better. How about Cater-waller? Or Catrina?

Hippo held up his. He'd taken it out of the jar and held it between his thumb and finger. "Mine is Godzilla," he said. "Mine can stomp all over yours!"

"It can't stomp," said Allison. She shook her red braids. She and Brett were partners. "It doesn't have any feet."

"Yes, it does," said Robin. "Look closer. Lots and lots of little tiny feet."

"What did you name yours?" asked Hippo, ignoring Robin.

"Cole," said Brett. "After my dog."

"Bor-ing," sang Hippo. He started to draw.

Robin and Zoey worked hard in their journals, drawing a picture of Marvin.

Zoey got up to get a drink. Robin admired the way Zoey's shoes went click-click-click.

"Tap shoes," said Zoey when she got back. "I took tap dancing at my old school."

"Ooh," said Robin.

"*Oui,*" said Zoey. "That's French for yes."

"Do you want to eat lunch with me?" asked Robin.

Zoey shook her head. "I already told Allison I'd eat with her," she said.

Disappointment settled over Robin as she ʰed Zoey click-click away.

ᵉlbowed her in the arm. "I'll eat ᵃid.

Chapter Five

Tap Shoes

"How was school today, Birdie?" asked Gramps.

Gramps had made pumpkin muffins. They were still warm. The kitchen smelled like cinnamon. Robin bit into a muffin.

"There's this new girl in my class," said Robin. "She can talk French and she wears lipstick. Well, lip gloss anyway. And tap shoes. Can I have some tap shoes?"

"Put it on your birthday list," said Gramps.

Her birthday was still two months. Practically summertime. Too long to

* * *

After dinner Robin made tap shoes.

"What are you doing?" asked Tamara as she passed Robin's room.

"Making tap shoes," said Robin.

"Weird," said Tamara. She ran downstairs. Probably to call a boy, thought Robin. Tamara was always doing stuff like that.

Robin went back to work. She glued bottle caps to the bottoms of her old Sunday school shoes. They clicked nicely when she walked.

* * *

The next day Robin wore her tap shoes to school. Click. Click.

Zoey was already in her seat. "Now we're twins," Robin whispered.

Zoey shook her head and pointed at her feet. She wore pink sneakers with daisies sewn on them.

Well, that's okay, thought Robin. We're still twins. Sort of.

"Class," said Miss Wing, "get out your caterpillar journals."

Zoey and Robin worked in their journals. Robin drew a picture of Marvin and labeled the parts.

Zoey wrote a caterpillar poem.

Robin couldn't wait to hear the tap shoes again. It was such a glamorous sound. She raised her hand.

"Can I get a drink?" she asked.

"*May* I get a drink," said Miss Wing.

"*May* I get a drink?" asked Robin.

Miss Wing nodded.

Click-clack. Clickety-clack went the bottle caps. Just like Zoey's.

Robin didn't notice the other kids watching. She got her drink and walked back. Click-clack. Clickety-clack.

She finished her journal. "May I get a drink?" she asked.

Miss Wing shook her head.

"Then may I go to the rest room?"

Miss Wing frowned, but nodded.

Click-clickety-click went the tap shoes, all the way across the room to the door and down the hall.

On the way back, Miss Wing was standing by the classroom door.

"May I have a word with you, Robin?" she asked. "In the hall?"

Suddenly Robin didn't feel so good.

"I couldn't help noticing that you had to leave your seat a lot today, Robin," said Miss Wing. "And I couldn't help noticing the noise you made. What makes that clicking sound when you walk?"

Robin held up her foot to show Miss Wing the bottle caps glued to the bottom.

"Tap shoes," she explained. "Like Zoey's."

Miss Wing frowned. "Then I'll tell you what I told Zoey. Tap shoes belong at home and in tap dancing class. Not in school."

She went back inside the room.

Robin's face felt hot. That must be why Zoey hadn't worn hers today. Robin sat down in the hall and tried to pry off the bottle caps. They wouldn't come off.

Robin went in and sat down. She tried to tip-toe so the bottle caps wouldn't click on the floor.

The next day Zoey wore glasses with rain-bow-striped frames. At sharing time she raised her hand.

"I went to the eye doctor and got new glasses," said Zoey. "I picked out the frames myself."

Miss Wing smiled. "We must be twins!" she said, pointing to her glasses. They had rainbow-striped frames, too.

Robin felt a small lurch in her tummy. If Miss Wing and Zoey were twins, what was Robin?

She couldn't be twins with Zoey because she didn't have tap shoes. She couldn't be twins with Miss Wing because Miss Wing never wore the red sneakers anymore. Robin was left out, that's what she was.

All through caterpillar study she worked quietly. She didn't even want to look at Zoey. Zoey had rainbow-striped glasses. Zoey had tap shoes. Zoey could speak French. If only Zoey liked her!

But Robin knew there was nothing special about her to make Zoey notice her.

She had plain hair. She had plain eyes. She had plain shoes. Nothing special at all.

That night Robin helped with dinner. Gramps mashed the potatoes. Tamara put the pork chops on a plate. Robin set the beets on the table.

"Give your mother a chance to put her feet up," said Gramps.

Mom smiled and kicked off her shoes. She put her feet up on the cozy footstool and opened her bag of knitting.

"You're supposed to be resting," said Tamara. "Not knitting."

"This is restful," said Mom. "It was a long day."

At dinner Robin asked, "Can I get glasses?"

"Glasses!" said Mom. "Whatever for? Are you having trouble seeing the board?"

"No," said Robin.

"You don't need glasses," said Mom. "Our family has excellent eyesight."

"Can I get contacts?" asked Tamara.

"Contacts!" said Mom. "Are *you* having trouble seeing the board?"

"No," said Tamara. "But with contacts you can have turquoise eyes, or violet eyes, or even red-striped eyes. Cool. There's this boy at school . . ."

Robin tuned out. Once Tamara started talking about boys, there was no point listening to her.

Robin sighed and stirred her mashed potatoes with a fork. She loved it when the beets touched the mashed potatoes. Red beet juice ran into the potatoes and turned them pink. Mom would never let her get glasses. She'd have to think of something else.

Chapter Six

"I See Paris, I See France"

The next day Robin rooted around in her bottom drawer until she found her sunglasses. They weren't wraparound glasses or mirror glasses. Just plain sunglasses. Still, they were better than nothing.

Now she would be twins with Zoey *and* Miss Wing!

"*Très chic,*" said Zoey when she saw them. "That means they are cool."

Robin wore her glasses during circle time. Miss Wing read *Charlotte's Web*. Robin loved the story of the pig and spider. But even sitting close, she couldn't see the pictures through the dark glass. And leaving the circle, she tripped over Jamie's feet.

"Hey! Watch it!" said Jamie.

Miss Wing did not seem to think they were twins.

"Robin," said Miss Wing. "Sunglasses are for outside. Please put them in your backpack."

Robin felt sick. Wouldn't her teacher ever like her again? Miss Wing was so pretty! She was so smart. She was so cool! Why couldn't they be twins? Robin zipped her sunglasses into the front pocket of her backpack.

The next day Miss Wing held up a plastic jar. "Today we are going to measure our caterpillars," she told the class.

Robin liked the way Miss Wing looked this morning. She wore black pants and a red shirt. A dragon was painted across the top of the shirt. Her earrings were dragons, too. Her rainbow-striped glasses glittered in the light.

"Take your caterpillars out and lay them straight along the metric ruler," said Miss Wing.

Zoey nudged Robin.

"You do it," she said. "I don't want to touch it."

Robin opened the plastic jar. She picked up Marvin with her fingers. He wasn't slimy at all.

She was very gentle. He curled up a little. She set him down on the table.

Hippo held his caterpillar above his head and waved it at Zoey.

"Watch out! Godzilla's going to crush you!"

"EEEEK!" yelled Zoey.

"Knock it off," said Robin. She gave Hippo a shove.

He bumped the table.

Marvin rolled off.

"Now look what you've done!" said Robin. "Where's Marvin?"

She got down on her hands and knees to look for him. He wasn't on the floor. She looked on the table. He wasn't there, either. Where could he be?

Miss Wing came over. "What's going on?" she asked.

Zoey had a very funny look on her face.

"We can't find Marvin," said Robin.

Zoey began to wiggle up and down. "I think I know where Marvin is," she whispered.

Robin looked at Zoey. Her face was pale. She hopped from leg to leg.

Marvin was in Zoey's pants!

"I'll help," yelled Robin. She tugged the waistband of Zoey's pants. The elastic broke and Zoey's pants slid down around her ankles.

Robin saw something on the floor by Zoey's foot. It looked like a piece of fuzz.

"Marvin!" Robin cried. She picked him up and put him back in the jar. She was so relieved, she didn't notice Zoey. "It's okay, he's all right," Robin started to say. Then she looked up.

Zoey's underpants were printed with yellow ducks. Zoey's face was beet red.

The class stared at Zoey's underwear. Zoey stared at Robin in horror.

"I see Paris! I see France! I see Zoey's underpants!" chanted Hippo. He pointed at Zoey.

Zoey grabbed her pants and pulled them back up, but it was too late. The whole class laughed.

Zoey's eyes filled with tears. She clutched the waistband of her pants. "How could you!" she snapped.

"I was just trying to help," said Robin. Her throat felt tight.

"Come with me, dear," said Miss Wing to Zoey. "I have a safety pin in my desk."

Zoey glared at Robin as she walked with Miss Wing. Robin thought Miss Wing glared, too.

"Ooh," said Zoey, when she got back. Her pants were pinned up with a safety pin. Her lip was shaking. Her eyes looked all watery. "That was stressful."

Robin looked at Marvin. He was curled up in a jar. "It was stressful for Marvin, too," she said.

Zoey tossed her head. "I don't care. It was all your fault, Robin. You and that stupid caterpillar. I don't want to be your partner anymore."

Without another word she gathered up her backpack and caterpillar journal and went to sit with Jamie and Charly.

Robin felt lost. Now Zoey was mad at her. Miss Wing thought she was a bad kid. What was next?

Hippo leaned over.

"I'm your caterpillar partner now," he said. "I know! Let's put Godzilla and Marvin into the same jar. Make 'em fight! I'll bet Godzilla will stomp all over Marvin!"

Robin let out a deep breath. Great. Now she was stuck with Hippo.

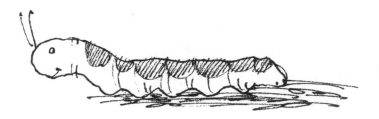

Chapter Seven

The Yard Sale

On Saturday Robin spent the day with Gramps. Mom had to work an extra shift and Tamara was at a soccer game.

On Saturdays Robin and Gramps went to yard sales. It was their favorite thing to do.

Robin carried her red purse. She had two whole dollars to spend. She'd saved the money from returning pop cans.

"Who knows what treasures we might find?" said Gramps.

Robin loved the way Gramps smelled like peppermints and pipe tobacco. He didn't smoke anymore ("Bad for the lungs," he said) but he still kept his favorite pipe in the pocket of his flannel shirt, just to chew on.

"Gramps," said Robin while they were in the car together.

"Yes, Birdie?"

"I have a problem."

"A home problem or a school problem?"

"School problem." Robin sighed. "A big school problem."

"Lay it on me, Birdie," said Gramps. He pulled the car over and shut off the engine. He turned to look at Robin. His eyes were blue and his beard was gray.

"There's this girl in my class named Zoey. And she's really cool. She has pierced ears and glasses and pink lip gloss."

"Sounds interesting."

"Oh, and she can speak French, too. Can I take French lessons?"

"Put it on—"

"My birthday list, I know. I know." Robin picked a piece of skin off her finger. She always did that when she was worried. It was her bad habit.

"I wanted to be friends, but now she doesn't like me." Robin told about the underwear. "I said I was sorry, but she wouldn't listen."

Gramps roughed up her hair. "Give her time, Birdie. She'll get over it."

Robin sighed. Would Zoey get over it?

They drove up the street to the next sale.

There was a lady behind a table. She sat in a green and white lawn chair. In front of her was a cash register.

Gramps browsed a table of mismatched china. Robin looked around.

Gramps found a saucer with a blue pattern. "Blue willow," he whispered to Robin. "Let me see how much she wants."

Robin spotted a box of old clothes.

"Might be something vintage in here," she said.

"You go right ahead," he told her.

Robin dug through the box. It was like digging for treasure. She pulled up a little black purse on a chain. A yellow scarf. A knit cap with fuzzy balls. Down in the very bottom of the box was a pair of eyeglasses.

Robin put them on. They slipped down her nose a little bit. They made the world seem all wavy, like looking through the window when it's raining or looking through a glass of water. The frames were not rainbow striped. They were black and shaped like cat's eyes. In each pointed corner were three rhinestones. Or there should have been three rhinestones. One was missing.

Robin took it up to the lady in the lawn chair. "How much for these?" she asked shyly.

"Dollar and a quarter," said the lady. She smiled at Robin. "Going to play dress up?"

"Sort of," said Robin. She gave the lady two dollars. The lady counted back three quarters and handed Robin the glasses.

Maybe there was a way to make Zoey and Miss Wing like her after all.

Chapter Eight

Four-eyed Twins

Robin wore the cat's eye glasses to school the next day. What would Miss Wing say when she saw them? Now they would be twins. What would Zoey think? Would she still be mad? Robin hoped not.

But when she got to school, Zoey was absent. Too bad. Robin really wanted to show Zoey her glasses. But a teensy part of Robin was relieved. Because maybe Zoey was still mad.

During sharing Robin raised her hand.

"Yes, Robin?" said Miss Wing.

"I have new glasses," said Robin.

It wasn't quite a lie. They were new. New to Robin, anyway. And she did have them.

"We must be twins!" said Miss Wing.

Robin's heart felt as light as a butterfly. She didn't need tap shoes. She didn't need pierced ears. She and Miss Wing were twins.

Robin worked on her caterpillar journal. Hippo tapped on the table with his pencil. "Godzilla is bigger than Marvin," he whispered. Robin ignored him.

She wore her new glasses. The glass made it hard to write. Everything looked sort of wavy.

"Cattterpilllars groe fsst," wrote Robin. It didn't look right. Were the words spelled wrong? She erased and tried again. Maybe she should take her glasses off. Maybe it would be easier to write.

"I like your glasses," whispered Allison, sitting behind her. "They make you look smart."

That decided it. Whether they made things hard to see or not, the glasses stayed on.

All day long Robin was happy. Happy that she and Miss Wing were friends again. Happy that the glasses made her look smart.

The next day Zoey was back. She brought her backpack and journal over to Robin's table.

"Miss Wing said I have to be your partner," said Zoey. "I said I guess so." She gave Robin a stern look. "But don't ever, ever do that again!"

Robin was glad Zoey was back. Robin took the glasses out of her backpack and put them on. "Look!" she said. "We're twins!"

Zoey looked. Slowly she shook her head.

"No," she said. "Twins match. Like me and Miss Wing. Those glasses don't have rainbow stripes. They're just plain black."

Robin's face got hot. Her throat hurt. Zoey was right. They weren't twins, and Robin and Miss Wing weren't twins, either.

Just then Hippo leaned across the table. He'd been listening.

"Twins?" he said. "Yeah, right. Goggle-eye twins! Four eyes plus four eyes equals eight eyes!"

Robin thought she might cry.

"Four eyes?" yelled Zoey. Her voice was so loud, everyone stopped to look at her. Even Allison stopped writing.

"Four eyes?" Zoey repeated. She stood up and scowled. "Well, four eyes are better than two, half brain.

"Besides," she added, "we are too twins. You're just jealous." She flung her arm around Robin's shoulders and marched out to recess.

Robin couldn't believe her luck. All recess Zoey stayed with her.

"We'll be best friends," whispered Zoey. "I'll teach you to talk French. You can borrow my tap shoes."

She glared in Hippo's direction. "And we'll swear a blood pact not to like that Hippo kid. That's for sure."

"What's a blood pact?" whispered Robin. It didn't sound good.

"I cut my finger and you cut yours. We mingle our blood and promise to be best friends and Hippo's worst nightmare."

"I don't know," said Robin. She didn't like blood. She didn't want to cut her finger.

Zoey's eyes flashed behind her glasses.

For just a moment Robin was afraid. Maybe they wouldn't be friends?

Then Zoey smiled.

"We'll do a spit pact then," she said. "That's what we did at my other school."

Zoey spit on her index finger. Robin spit on hers. They touched fingers together. "Now we're best friends until the end of time," said Zoey. "No one can break us up."

Robin was thrilled. At last she was friends with the amazing Zoey! All because of the glasses. Robin blinked behind the wavy glass. She couldn't wait to tell Gramps.

But when she got on the bus to go home, Robin realized she couldn't tell Gramps without telling about the glasses. She didn't know why, but somehow she didn't want Mom or Gramps to know that she was wearing yard sale glasses at school.

She tucked them into her backpack. What Mom and Gramps didn't know wouldn't hurt them, she thought.

Chapter Nine

Marvin Moves On

"Miss Wing! Come quickly!" yelled Hippo the next day at school. "Godzilla is gone!"

Miss Wing came over to Hippo's table.

"Oh, my!" she cried. "He's turned into a chrysalis! All right, Hippo!" She gave Hippo a high five. In her excitement, she forgot to call him Eric.

All the class gathered around. Instead of a caterpillar, there was a shiny blob hanging from the paper that covered Hippo's jar. It looked like a bean pod with bumps, but it was the wrong color.

"Class," said Miss Wing, "this is a chrysalis. It's the pupae stage of the butterfly. In a week or so, Godzilla will emerge as an adult insect. A butterfly."

"Wow," said Hippo. He was grinning so hard his eyes scrinched up.

"When will Marvin make his chrysalis?" asked Zoey.

"All the caterpillars will become pupas soon," said Miss Wing. "It's time to build our flight cages. We'll put the pupae inside and wait for them to emerge."

Each table group worked on a butterfly cage. Hippo, Zoey, and Robin used a big cardboard box. Robin cut one side out to make a window so they'd be able to see the butterflies. Hippo made a flap in back so they'd be able to put fresh sugar water in the cage every day.

"Hey!" said Zoey, looking up from the drawing she was doing. "Where are your glasses?"

Robin touched her face. Her glasses! She'd forgotten to put them on. She quickly pulled them out of her backpack. "Here they are!"

"Good," said Zoey. She went back to work.

Robin sighed. She'd have to be careful not to forget them again. What if Zoey decided they weren't twins anymore? What if Zoey decided they weren't best friends?

"Wow," said Hippo again. "Godzilla is the first one." He began to chant. "I'm number one! I'm number one!"

"Knock it off, Hippo," said Robin. But she didn't say it meanly. She was happy for him. Soon Marvin would make a chrysalis, too.

At recess she played with Zoey. Hippo came over, too. They hung upside down on the monkey bars, Zoey on one side, Hippo on the other, and Robin in the middle.

"That Hippo kid isn't so bad," said Zoey afterward.

The next day Hippo, Zoey, and Robin finished the butterfly cage. They covered the whole box with pictures of flowers. Then they wrapped it in clear plastic wrap, except for the air holes and the back door. Carefully Miss Wing moved the paper that held Godzilla to the cage.

Marvin was still a caterpillar. He shed his skin again. He was a big fat caterpillar now.

Allison and Brett's caterpillar became a chrysalis. They moved it to their flight cage. Charly and Jamie's changed, too.

One by one, all the caterpillars changed into chrysalises.

Soon only Marvin was left.

"When, oh, when," sang Robin softly. "When will he spin?" She knew caterpillars didn't spin cocoons like moths, but "chrysalis" didn't sound as good.

Finally Marvin stopped eating. Robin watched him. The glasses made him look too wavy, so she pulled them down on her nose and looked over the top.

Marvin inched his way to the top of the jar.

"Miss Wing!" yelled Robin. "Come quick!"

Miss Wing dashed over. That was another thing Robin loved about Miss Wing. She was there when you needed her.

All the kids crowded around.

Marvin hung on the paper lid of the jar. He curled his body into a J shape.

"He's ready!" yelled Robin. "He's changing!"

It looked like Marvin's skin was splitting. Underneath was all shiny and hard. He wasn't fuzzy anymore. Now he looked like all the others.

"Ick," said Zoey. But her eyes were shining.

Carefully Miss Wing moved him to the butterfly cage with Godzilla. Robin let her breath out. She hadn't even known she'd been holding it.

"Congratulations," said Miss Wing. She hugged Robin and Zoey. "In about a week you'll have a butterfly."

Chapter Ten

Pizza Pit Stop

"Hurry up, Robin!" called Tamara.

Robin grabbed her red purse and her sweater. She ran down the stairs to the car. It was Friday night. They were going out for pizza.

Mom drove. Gramps sat in front. Robin slid into the backseat next to Tamara.

Pizza Pit Stop was Robin's favorite place. The tables looked like race cars. The clerks wore black-and-white shirts checked like racing flags. Right in the middle of the restaurant was a real race car.

Best of all were the video games. Robin's favorite was Race Car Rampage. She had seven quarters saved up in her red purse.

Pizza Pit Stop was crowded. Video games blinked and beeped. Loud music played. Over all the noise came the loudspeaker: "Order number eighty-one. Number eighty-one."

The whole place smelled of garlic and cheese. It was hot and crowded and noisy. Robin loved it. They found a table and slid onto the benches.

"Hey, Robin!" called a voice.

Robin looked around. Hippo stuck his thumbs in his ears and wiggled his fingers.

That Hippo! What would he do next?

"What are you doing here?" she asked.

"It's a free country," said Hippo. "Gotta go. My pizza's up!"

He ran off to another table.

"Can I play the games now?" Robin asked, bouncing up and down.

"Me, too?" asked Tamara.

"Just a minute," said Mom. "What does everybody want? Can we all agree this time?"

They couldn't agree. Robin wanted pine-apple. Tamara wanted pepperoni. Gramps hated pineapple and loved anchovies. No one else would eat anchovies. Mom didn't want any meat. No one else wanted vegetables.

Mom scribbled notes on an envelope. "Let's see, that's one medium, half anchovies, half pepperoni with extra cheese. Another medium, half veggie, half ham and pineapple. Two salads. Four root beers. Got it." She sighed. "That's an awful lot of pizza for four people."

Gramps patted her arm. "We can eat left-overs for lunch tomorrow."

"Yum!" said Robin. "Cold pizza for lunch!"

"Can we go now?" asked Tamara.

Mom went to the counter to order. Gramps stayed at the table to save their places. Robin and Tamara left for the games. Robin took her purse with the seven quarters.

Luckily no one else was playing Race Car Rampage. Robin dropped a quarter into the slot. Instead of a joystick, the game had a steering wheel. Robin loved to careen around corners with the tires squealing.

She pretended she was in a real race. She wasn't aware of anyone else until the game was over. Then she sighed and looked around.

Maybe she could catch a stuffed animal with the giant claw. The purple frog looked pretty cute.

Just then she saw Zoey. She wore a pink shirt.

"Zoey! Over here!" Robin called. Zoey turned. Light glinted off her glasses.

Oh, no! Glasses! Robin ducked around the car. She pulled her glasses out of her purse and put them on.

Now everything looked wavy. "Hi! Zoey!" she called to a pink blur.

"Robin?" The girl in pink came over. It wasn't Zoey. It was Tamara!

Robin whipped off the glasses and held them behind her back. Her face felt hot.

Tamara gave Robin a funny look. "You're weird," she said. "Come on. Our pizza's ready."

"I'm coming." Zoey was still by the counter. Without the glasses, Robin could see her just fine.

When Tamara left, Robin shoved her glasses back on. Zoey turned around. Robin waved. Zoey waved back.

At least Robin *thought* it was Zoey.

Robin headed for the table, taking off the glasses and stashing them in her purse. What good luck she'd had them with her! It would have been awful if Zoey had seen her without glasses.

Just then the worst thing happened. The absolute worst thing in the world. Hippo! He was standing right by the race car! Had he seen her?

Hippo turned. He circled his thumb and forefingers, held them to his eyes, and peered through. Glasses!

He'd seen her put the glasses on. He'd seen her take the glasses off. He knew she didn't really need glasses.

Robin was caught! Would he tell?

She started forward, but Hippo ducked behind the car.

Tamara grabbed her arm. "What are you waiting for?" she asked. "I'm starving! Let's eat."

Reluctantly Robin let herself be pulled toward the table.

She sat down. The pizza smelled delicious, but Robin couldn't eat. Close calls were exhausting.

"What did you name yours?" asked Hippo, ignoring Robin.

"Cole," said Brett. "After my dog."

"Bor-ing," sang Hippo. He started to draw.

Robin and Zoey worked hard in their journals, drawing a picture of Marvin.

Zoey got up to get a drink. Robin admired the way Zoey's shoes went click-click-click.

"Tap shoes," said Zoey when she got back. "I took tap dancing at my old school."

"Ooh," said Robin.

"*Oui,*" said Zoey. "That's French for yes."

"Do you want to eat lunch with me?" asked Robin.

Zoey shook her head. "I already told Allison I'd eat with her," she said.

Disappointment settled over Robin as she watched Zoey click-click away.

Hippo elbowed her in the arm. "I'll eat with you!" he said.

That Hippo!

Chapter Five

Tap Shoes

"How was school today, Birdie?" asked Gramps.

Gramps had made pumpkin muffins. They were still warm. The kitchen smelled like cinnamon. Robin bit into a muffin.

"There's this new girl in my class," said Robin. "She can talk French and she wears lipstick. Well, lip gloss anyway. And tap shoes. Can I have some tap shoes?"

"Put it on your birthday list," said Gramps.

Her birthday was still two months away. Practically summertime. Too long to wait.

* * *

Chapter Eleven

The Secret

The next week was horrible.

Hippo knew her secret. When would he tell?

But the days went by, and Hippo didn't say anything.

At lunchtime Robin sat with Zoey. Across the room Hippo put his circled fingers up to his eyes and peered through. Glasses.

At recess Zoey and Robin played hopscotch. Hippo watched from across the playground. He circled his fingers and stared. Glasses.

In the library Zoey and Robin checked out *Charlotte's Web*. Hippo peered between circled fingers. Glasses.

It drove her crazy! She wanted to kick him, or scream, or run away. It was like playing with a time bomb. *Tick, tick, tick.* He was going to tell. But when?

Every day Robin looked into the butterfly cage. Marvin and Godzilla hung from the top. Inside the chrysalises they were busy changing into butterflies, Robin knew. But on the outside, they were quiet and still.

Just like her.

On the outside she looked calm. She went to school, played with Zoey, did her work. But inside butterflies tap danced in her stomach.

And every time Hippo saw her, he made glasses with his fingers.

Thursday afternoon. Marvin and Godzilla had been hanging in the butterfly cage for a week.

"It won't be long now," said Miss Wing as she lined everyone up to go home.

Zoey went to the closet to get her backpack. Robin stayed at the table to finish her math. She wore the glasses.

Mom walked in. At first Robin didn't recognize her. She was just a blurry shape.

The blur got closer. Robin jumped up. "Mom!" she cried. "What are you doing here?"

Mom smiled. "I got off work early," she said. "I need more yarn to finish your vest. How about coming with me?"

"Goody!" said Robin. "Can we stop for ice cream?" she asked. Mom nodded, then looked at her strangely.

Just then Hippo jabbed her in the arm with his elbow.

"Knock it off, Hippo," Robin said.

Hippo elbowed her again. "The glasses, dummy!" he hissed.

The glasses! She yanked them off and held them behind her.

Mom gave her a funny look.

"Get your backpack, Robin," she said. She went over to Miss Wing. Robin saw her say something. They both turned and looked at Robin. Her face grew hot. What were they saying?

And why had Hippo warned her instead of telling? She turned to ask him, but she was too late. He'd vanished out the door.

* * *

* * *

That night Robin set the table for dinner. "Forks on the left, spoons on the right," she murmured. "What's for dinner, Gramps?"

"Bean soup," said Gramps. Robin sighed. She didn't like bean soup.

"Corn bread, too," added Gramps. "With butter and honey."

Robin cheered up. She liked to dribble honey on crumbly warm corn bread. It tasted like cake.

"Soup's on!" called Gramps.

Mom came in. She held Robin's vest. "It's done!" she said. "Here, try it on."

Robin slipped the vest on over her T-shirt. It was robin's egg blue, with yellow and white daisies.

"It's beautiful!" Robin said. She flung her arms around Mom and kissed her. "Thank you!"

Robin took the blue vest off and folded it up. She didn't want to stain it.

Mom and Robin sat down. Gramps dished up. Robin helped herself to a piece of corn bread.

Tamara slid into her chair, scowling.

"What's the matter?" asked Robin.

"Bad day," said Tamara.

"Why was it a bad day?" asked Mom.

Tamara heaved a big sigh. She put her elbows on the table. "Holly and I wanted to play a joke on Emmy. We pretended my ankle was sprained. I limped around. Emmy really fell for it! She got me ice from the office. She bought me a soda. She even offered to carry my lunch tray in the cafeteria."

Tamara poked at her soup. "But when she found out we were just teasing, she was really mad."

Tamara sighed again. "She told Mrs. Zachary, our English teacher. And Mrs. Zachary took Emmy's side! Mrs. Zachary said we lied. I don't understand why. We didn't say anything!"

Robin stopped with the spoon halfway to her mouth. Her stomach felt suddenly strange.

Mom looked thoughtful. "Sometimes you can lie with actions, sweetie. Like pretending something is true when it's not. That's a kind of lie."

Robin stirred her beans. Like if you pretend you wear glasses and you don't? she wondered.

"Oh, what a tangled web we weave, When first we practice to deceive," quoted Gramps. He took a second helping of soup. While everyone else had been talking, he'd been eating.

"What does that mean?" asked Robin.

"Lies get worse," said Mom. "If you tell one, you sometimes have to tell another and another. To cover up the first one. They spin out of control."

Robin's throat felt tight. A tangled web. Like the little lie she told Miss Wing about the glasses. Now she was lying to Zoey and Mom and Gramps. Even to the whole class.

"What do I do now?" asked Tamara. "I don't want Emmy to be mad at me."

"Apologies usually work," Mom said.

Tamara brightened up. "I could phone her after dinner," she said. "And tell her I'm sorry. And that I won't do it again." She began to eat.

Robin's corn bread suddenly tasted like cardboard.

"May I be excused?" she asked. She wanted to be alone. To think.

Chapter Twelve

Godzilla the Butterfly

Robin sat on the edge of her bed. She picked at the skin on the side of her thumb. It was a sore place. She knew she shouldn't pick it, but she did sometimes. When she was worried.

She was worried now.

You could tell a lie by not saying anything at all.

She thought about how the glasses made her look smart. How they made her twins with Miss Wing and Zoey. How hard they were to see through. How hard it was to keep pretending.

She had snatched off the glasses when Mom came to pick her up. Why didn't she

71

want Mom to see her in the glasses? She knew the answer to that.

Because all the time, in her heart, she knew she was lying.

What had Mom said? "Apologies usually work"?

Maybe it was time for a new plan.

The next day Robin woke up late. Her head hurt. Maybe she was sick? Maybe she shouldn't go to school?

No, that was another kind of lie.

Her feet dragged as she walked to the bus stop. She wore her red sneakers for courage. But they weren't helping.

The bus squealed to a stop. The doors creaked open. Robin plopped into a seat. The doors clanged shut. The bus rumbled along.

Hippo was across the aisle. He pointed.

"Where's the glasses, four eyes?" he said.

"You know I don't really wear glasses," said Robin. "Why did you keep my secret?"

Hippo shrugged. "I don't know," he said. He turned and stared out the bus window.

The back of his neck was red. Even the backs of his ears were red. She remembered how she and Zoey and Hippo had worked on the butterfly cage together. How they had hung upside down on the monkey bars. Did Hippo keep her secret so she would be his friend?

Maybe he'd been her friend all along and she never knew.

Miss Wing opened the door to the classroom. All the kids pushed inside. Except Robin.

"Miss Wing," said Robin. "Can I talk to you? In the hall?" Better do it and get it over with, she thought.

"Sure thing," said Miss Wing.

Robin swallowed. She looked at her red sneakers. She picked at the skin on her thumb.

Then she held out the yard sale glasses. "I didn't mean to be lying," she said. "But I don't really wear glasses. I bought them at a yard sale. I just wanted to be twins with you."

Miss Wing took the glasses. She turned them over and over in her hands. Robin looked at the floor. She waited for Miss Wing to say she was disappointed. Or give her a time out. Or maybe even send her to the principal.

But Miss Wing didn't. When Robin finally had the courage to look up, she was surprised.

Miss Wing was laughing! Robin couldn't believe it.

"Robin," said Miss Wing, "you don't have to wear glasses for us to be twins. We can be *Charlotte's Web* twins. We can be red sneaker twins. We can be butterfly twins." She reached out and gave Robin a hug.

Just then Zoey ran out. "Miss Wing! Come quick! Something's happening!"

Robin and Miss Wing followed Zoey to the butterfly cage. Robin looked at it without the glasses. The cage was perfectly clear. It didn't look blurry or fuzzy or wavy. It was a relief to see.

"It's Godzilla!" yelled Hippo. The chrysalis was splitting open.

For one moment Robin felt a twinge of envy. Why couldn't Marvin be first? Then she squashed it down deep inside.

"That's cool, Hippo," she said. She smiled.

Hippo grinned so hard his eyes scrinched up. He wiggled his ears.

The butterfly used its front legs to push itself out. Then it perched on the edge of the old, empty chrysalis. The class watched the butterfly fan its wings up and down.

"It's pumping blood into its wings," said Miss Wing. "So it will be able to fly."

The wings were orange and brown and yellow. The butterfly had six delicate black legs and two skinny black antennae.

"*Très belle*," whispered Zoey. "It's beautiful." Her eyes were big behind her glasses.

It was beautiful, thought Robin. But she couldn't watch all day. There was something she needed to do.

Robin touched Zoey's arm. "Zoey," she whispered. "I need to talk to you." They moved away from the class, all crowded around the butterfly cage.

"Zoey. I don't really wear glasses. I just wanted you to like me." Robin spit it all out in a rush. To her surprise it was easier to say a second time.

Zoey narrowed her eyes. She folded her mouth into a straight line. Her eyebrows came together above the rainbow-striped glasses. Her face looked like a storm cloud.

Here it comes, thought Robin. She steadied herself to bear the blast of Zoey's anger.

"You did that?" Zoey asked. "You wore glasses so I'd like you?"

To Robin's surprise, Zoey smiled. "But I do like you! I always liked you! You smiled at me the first day I came. You looked so friendly. I wanted to be your friend, too."

Robin sighed. "Then we're still best friends?" she asked hopefully.

"*Oui,*" said Zoey. She pointed to her feet.

Robin couldn't believe it. Zoey was wearing red high-top lace-up sneakers.

"We're twins," said Zoey.

Chapter Thirteen

Fly Free, Marvin

A few days later Miss Wing's class stood in the school garden. The sun was hot. Only a few puffy white clouds floated in the sky.

Robin wore her new blue vest.

"That's pretty," said Zoey when she saw it. "Maybe your mom would make me one, too."

"She could, I'll bet. I'll ask her." Robin grinned at her best friend.

Robin shifted from one foot to another. She couldn't wait. Today the class was going to release Marvin, Godzilla, and the rest of the butterflies.

The garden was bright with flowers. Red, pink, yellow, and orange. Miss Wing had told them butterflies like bright colors.

There was even a special bush with purple flowers. "A butterfly bush," said Miss Wing.

Hippo stood next to Robin and Zoey. He held their butterfly cage. Allison and Brett held the cage with their butterfly in it. The rest of the kids held their cages, too.

Miss Wing read a poem Zoey had written:

"Fly free, butterfly,
Fly to the flowers.
Let the breeze cool your wings.
Let the sun warm you.
Mate and lay eggs.
New caterpillars will hatch.
Fly free."

Robin squeezed Zoey's hand. "Good job," she said.

Then it was time to let the butterflies go.

Hippo put the cage on the ground. Zoey and Robin peeled off the plastic wrap. At first Marvin and Godzilla didn't want to come out.

They must have felt the sunshine because Godzilla flew out, followed by Marvin.

Robin let her breath out. It was so beautiful she thought she might cry. Then she heard Hippo softly chanting.

"I'm number one! I'm number one!"

Immediately she didn't feel like crying anymore. That Hippo! Always up to something.

"Knock it off, Hippo," she said. But she said it quietly. She wasn't really mad.

Godzilla landed on an orange daisy. Marvin fluttered over to a red petunia. Soon all the butterflies were out of the cages. The garden was alive with wings.

Marvin left the petunia, and floated overhead. "Fly free, Marvin," whispered Robin. As if he heard her, he flew up and up. Robin watched until he was just a speck in the blue, blue sky.

Robin looked at Hippo. He saw her looking and wiggled his ears at her. Robin looked at Zoey. She grinned and blinked behind the rainbow-striped glasses.

Robin smiled at both of them. Two best friends were even better than one.

"Meet us at the monkey bars at recess?" asked Zoey.

"You bet!" said Robin.

Tips on Caring for Butterflies

The butterflies that Miss Wing's class raised are a species called Painted Lady butterflies (Vanessa cardui). They are found throughout North America. Miss Wing ordered the caterpillars through a science supply store, but you can also collect caterpillars in the wild.

Caterpillars from a science store come with food. But if you find a caterpillar outside, you must be careful to collect the plant it was eating when you found it. Caterpillars will not eat just any plant. Each kind of caterpillar eats different plants.

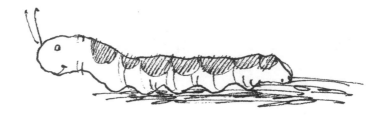

Caterpillars hatch from eggs, but the eggs are too small to be easily seen. After they hatch, they eat and eat for three to five days. Every few days, they shed their skin.

When the caterpillar is grown, it stops eating. It is ready to become a pupa, or chrysalis. Butterfly caterpillars do not spin cocoons. Only moth caterpillars do that.

The chrysalis stage lasts for about ten days. The chrysalis looks very still. You might wonder if it is dead. But be patient. The caterpillar is turning into a butterfly.

insert one end into one coffee can. Now put a bare branch in the tube for your insects to climb on. Put the other coffee can over the top. You can cut a little door in the screen so you can get into the cage to give the insects food or water. Fasten the door with a piece of wire or a paper clip.

When your butterfly hatches, feed it sugar water every day. But do not keep the butterfly too long.

Release your butterfly on a warm, sunny spring day. Butterflies like bright flowers so find a good place. You can write a poem like Zoey did, sing a song, or draw a picture to celebrate the release.

In about ten days, the butterfly emerges. Butterflies live two weeks to a month. They mate and lay eggs. That starts the cycle all over again.

You can make a butterfly cage from a cardboard box like Robin, Zoey, and Hippo did, or you can make a screen cage.

Here's how to make a screen cage:
Take two large coffee cans. Spray paint them any color you like. Let them dry.
Buy some screen from the hardware store. A piece about 15 inches wide by 30 inches long will be good. Roll the screen into a tube, and

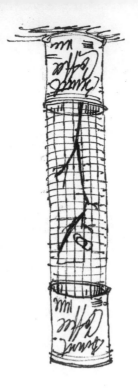